This

Buttons Family

book belongs to

_ _ _ _ _ _ _ _ _ _ _ _ _ _ _ _ _ _

_ _ _ _ _ _ _ _ _ _ _ _ _ _ _ _ _ _

Cherry and Charlie and Baby Lou,

We're the Buttons, we're just like you!

And every day there's something new

For Cherry and Charlie and Baby Lou!

First published 2012 by Walker Books Ltd
87 Vauxhall Walk, London SE11 5HJ

10 9 8 7 6 5 4 3 2 1

Text © 2012 Vivian French
Illustrations © 2012 Sue Heap

The right of Vivian French and Sue Heap to be identified as
author and illustrator respectively of this work has been
asserted by them in accordance with the Copyright, Designs
and Patents Act 1988

This book has been typeset in HVD Bodedo

Printed in China

British Library Cataloguing in
Publication Data: a catalogue record
for this book is available from
the British Library

ISBN 978-1-4063-2856-1

www.walker.co.uk

The Buttons Family
First Day
at Playschool

Vivian French

illustrated by
Sue Heap

WALKER BOOKS
AND SUBSIDIARIES
LONDON • BOSTON • SYDNEY • AUCKLAND

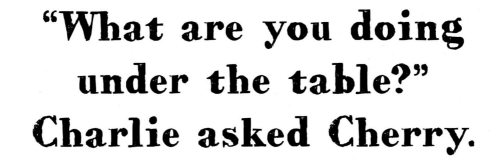

"What are you doing
under the table?"
Charlie asked Cherry.

"I don't WANT to go to playschool," Cherry said.

"I'll go!" Charlie shouted.

"Tell you what," Dad said,
"why don't we send Hoppy?"
Cherry stared at him. "But
Hoppy wants to stay with me."

"You're right," Dad said. "Hoppy told me he'll only go if a very grown-up girl goes with him. But he does want to play with friends and have fun. What a shame Hoppy can't go."

"I'm a grown-up girl!" said Cherry. "Hey, Hoppy," said Dad, "you can go to playschool after all." "Is it really fun?" Cherry asked. Dad nodded.

"I want to come!" said Charlie, as they set off.

At the gate Cherry stopped. "Are you SURE Hoppy wants to go to playschool?" she whispered. "He's a bit nervous," Dad said. "But you'll look after him. I'll just come in to meet your teacher."

The teacher was waiting in the hallway. "Hello – you must be Cherry! I'm Mrs Martin.

Hang your coat here and we'll go and meet the others."

"Sit next to Lizzie, Cherry," said Mrs Martin. "She'll look after you. Could you show her your hippo?"

Cherry made Hoppy wave. Mrs Martin smiled. "Now Cherry, are you ready to say goodbye to your daddy?"

Cherry gave Dad a goodbye hug, but her tummy felt very wobbly. Mrs Martin put an arm round her. "Do you like singing?" she asked.

They all sat in a circle and sang.

Then Mrs Martin read
a funny story about
a naughty puppy.

"Will you play with me?"
Lizzie whispered.

Cherry and Lizzie built
a castle together.

Then they painted pictures.

"What fantastic
pictures!" Mrs Martin said.
"Please," said Cherry, "can I go
to the toilet now?"

Cherry couldn't make the toilet flush. Lizzie showed her how. "Now we have to wash our hands," Lizzie said.

"Time for a snack!" said
Mrs Martin. "Cherry, would
you like to be a helper
and hand out the fruit?"

Cherry shook her head,
and a boy called Sam
took the plate.
Half way round
he tripped.

Mrs Martin tidied up, and fetched more fruit. This time Cherry helped Sam, and everybody clapped.

"What about some dressing-up?" said Mrs Martin. "I want to be a dragon," Lizzie said.

"I'll be a witch,"
said Sam.

"I'm a mummy
witch!" said Cherry.

Cherry, Lizzie and
Sam played until
Dad came in
with Charlie
and Baby Lou.

"Hello," Dad said. "Did Hoppy have a nice time?" "He had a LOVELY time!" Cherry hugged Dad. "You were right – playschool IS fun!"

There are six Buttons Family books to collect.
Which ones have you read?

New Shoes

Charlie's shoes are too tight!
He says he doesn't want
new ones, but what do
his toes say?

ISBN 978-1-4063-2855-4

Going to
the Doctor

Cherry's got a nasty cold.
How will Mum persuade
her to go to the doctor?

ISBN 978-1-4063-2857-8

Staying with Gran

Cherry, Charlie and Baby Lou have
never stayed with Gran on their
own before. Will Gran make sure
they feel at home?

ISBN 978-1-4063-2860-8

First Day
at Playschool

It's Cherry's first day
at playschool and she's
feeling a little shy.
How will she settle in?

ISBN 978-1-4063-2856-1

The
Babysitter

Mum and Dad are going out.
What do Cherry, Charlie
and Baby Lou think of the
new babysitter?

ISBN 978-1-4063-2858-5

Going to
the Dentist

It's time for the Buttons
to go to the dentist!
How will they get on at
their check-up?

ISBN 978-1-4063-2859-2

Available from all good booksellers